Fortune Hunters

Author: Jack Cull
Developer: Matt Finch
Editor: Jeff Harkness
S&W Conversion: Jeff Harkness
Art Direction: Casey Christofferson
Layout and Graphic Design: Charles A. Wright
Cover Design: Suzy Moseby
Cover Art: Colin Chan
Interior Art: Brett Blakely, Thuan Pham, Sid Quade, Erica Willey

ADVENTURES WORTH WINNING

FROG GOD GAMES

ISBN: 978-1-6656-0003-3

FROG GOD GAMES IS:

Bill Webb, Matthew J. Finch, Zach Glazar, Charles A. Wright, Edwin Nagy, Mike Badolato, John Barnhouse

Table of Contents

INTRODUCTION

The wonderful thing about non-player characters is that they give life to a game. Interesting NPCs make a game feel unique and special, especially when players get to interact with them (for better or worse). Not only that, but they help the players feel like they are playing in a real world, and that their actions matter to people. And over time, these characters will grow alongside the players, making the stakes of the adventure greater. A map and adventures are great, but the places need to be populated in order to make them feel alive.

The NPCs presented in this book each are given three stats blocks: one each for the equivalent level of 3, 6, and 10. While each character has a description, these different stat blocks are also accompanied by informational text about the characters at that point in their life (What was going on with them at Level 3? How are they different now at Level 6? And even more so at Level 10). We did this to allow you to have NPCs that can grow and advance along with the players. Perhaps an NPC is an early adversary for them, but they either get away, are allowed to live, or the players simply never engage them in combat to the death. You can now decide that enough time has gone by and use the next stat block iteration (3 to 6, or 6 to 10) to allow for a greater challenge. And who knows, with what the NPCs go through behind the scenes, perhaps they eventually become an ally. Or maybe an ally character becomes an enemy!

We decided to do the characters this way so that you have the tools to create a living, breathing world your players can interact with as it evolves through time. While it doesn't have to be done for every character, we wanted the NPCs here to help bring Cat's Cradle to life, to allow the players to connect with the people and places they come across. You are welcome to add onto the stories presented, omit what you don't like, or tie something in directly to your adventure or campaign to make everything feel even more connected. Whether they be allies to fight alongside, antagonists to stop, shopkeepers to interact with, or simply quest-givers for the party, each character is unique and contributes to the overall roleplaying experience.

ARIVER KYDAM

This tall, sallow-skinned young human knight holds himself rigidly in his ill-fitting plate armor. His shoulder-length greasy black hair frames his gaunt, hawk-nosed face as he glares as the "plebs" that occupy the street around him. He rests his gauntleted hand on the hilt of his bastard sword, waiting for an excuse to draw his blade and declare a duel against anyone who dares challenges him.

At 3rd Level: The third son of a local noble family, Ariver Kydam was born with a silver spoon in his mouth, and he loves to pull his noble birth rank whenever he can, typically demanding either first refusals or for preferential treatment. Flanking him at all times are a few of his friends that he uses as backup when he hopes to intimidate those who get in his way or who have something he wants. His stuck-up arrogance is known the instant words come out of his mouth, usually in the form of an insult or snide comment. In addition, Ariver can often be found observing the scene of a crime the local guards are investigating, although it is never from the standpoint of having any sympathy for the victim(s). Instead, he enjoys seeing the aftermath of the risky and dangerous lifestyle that criminals lead, and while he would never socialize with them openly, wishes to have a connection with the criminal underworld.

At 6th Level: Humiliated from a previous encounter with a group of do-gooders, Ser Kydam began looking for an extra edge in combat, more than simply his childhood friends to support him in battle. Not only has he improved his overall combat prowess, but Ariver has greased the palms of some local guardsmen to "shake down" his adversaries before any physical engagement. In addition, he has been able to use his increasing noble status to be the legitimate front for the shady dealings of a smuggling-focused thieves guild known as the "Wharf Rats" that deals out of Old Town and the Docks. Because of this, Ariver can call upon a half dozen rogue thugs that shadow him throughout town to join in any conflict he engages in. He does not ever join in any of the smuggling or thieving enterprises, but is always hungry to hear the nitty gritty details once the venture is complete.

At 9th Level: Ariver Kydam has become a noble of the court under Baron Scale within Cat's Cradle and the area around it, having a small keep in a province a few miles from the city proper. He has amassed a great deal of wealth from his criminal connections, and due to the fact that he had his two older brothers assassinated, he was assured to acquire his inherited position when his parents died. Since his severe scarring and disfigurement from a previous fight with troublesome "good" adversaries, Ariver has become a

bitter, jealous, and short-fused man, Lord Kydam primarily stays in his keep but commands a small military force that patrols his lands and enforces his iron-fisted rule. His criminal connections have also expanded: not only has the Wharf Rats smuggling organization grown in their enterprise in the city, but Ariver has known ties with the Crimson Skull pirates, the Crystal Husk witch coven from deep within the Forest of Cantricle, and even the Black Tongue assassins that work out of the city of Voles to the North.

Ariver Kydam, Male Human (Ftr3): HP 19; AC 5[14]; **Atk** bastard sword (1d8+2) or longbow x2 (1d6); **Move** 12; **Save** 12; **AL** C; **CL/XP** 3/60; **Special:** +1 to hit and damage strength bonus, multiple attacks (3) vs. creatures with 1 or fewer HD, summon reinforcements (1/day, 1d4+1 commoners). **Equipment:** chainmail, bastard sword, longbow, 20 arrows.

Ariver Kydam, Male Human (Ftr6): HP 42; AC 3[16]; **Atk** *+1 bastard sword* (1d8+4) or longbow x2 (1d6); **Move** 12; **Save** 9; **AL** C; **CL/XP** 6/400; **Special:** +1 to hit and damage strength bonus, multiple attacks (6) vs. creatures with 1 or fewer HD, summon reinforcements (1/day, 1d6+1 city guards). **Equipment:** plate mail, *+1 bastard sword*, longbow, 20 arrows.

Ariver Kydam, Male Human (Ftr10): HP 63; AC 2[17]; **Atk** *+1 bastard sword* (1d8+4) or longbow x2 (1d6); **Move** 12; **Save** 5; **AL** C; **CL/XP** 10/1400; **Special:** +1 to hit and damage strength bonus, multiple attacks (10) vs. creatures with 1 or fewer HD, summon reinforcements (1/day, 2d6 bandits). **Equipment:** *+1 plate mail*, *+1 bastard sword*, longbow, 20 arrows.

Note: Ariver can use his influence to get himself out of any unfavorable criminal political or social enterprise he may or may not be caught being involved in. It is up to your discretion as to how many times this ability can be used and its overall extent.

Commoners, Male or Female Humans (1d4+1): HD 1d6hp; AC 9[10]; **Atk** weapon (1d6); **Move** 12; **Save** 18; **AL** Any; **CL/XP** B/10; **Special:** none. (*Monstrosities* 254)

City Guards, Male or Female Humans (1d6+1): HD 1; AC 7[12]; **Atk** weapon (1d8); **Move** 12; **Save** 17; **AL** Any; **CL/XP** 1/15; **Special:** none. (*Monstrosities* 257)

Bandits, Male or Female Humans (2d6): HD 1; AC 7[12]; **Atk** weapon (1d8); **Move** 12; **Save** 17; **AL** C; **CL/XP** 1/15; **Special:** none. (*Monstrosities* 254)

AULRICH STEELSPADE

The brow of the dark-skinned dwarven proprietor cannot help but furrow as he observes the crowd of individuals occupying his establishment. The owner of The Rebellious Boggart Tavern and Game Hall stands confidently with his hands firmly on the second-floor railing as he stares over it at the ground floor below. Both his slicked-back black hair and long, braided Bandholz beard are groomed perfectly, matching his freshly laundered and pressed nobleman attire, perfectly tailored to fit his wide muscular frame. The glint of a mithril chain shirt can be spotted from his open shirt, and while a scimitar is strapped to his belt, a warhammer leans nearby within arm's reach.

At 3rd Level: Aulrich Steelspade is a gruff, foul-mouthed dwarf originally from the areas around the city of Voles to the North. He doesn't speak to anyone about the details of his youth, but it has been gathered over the years that he is on the run and hunted. Through the random anecdotes he grumbles off from time to time, many have theorized that it either included a mighty debt, a catastrophic fire, or a great number of people killed (perhaps even all three!). Whatever the case may be, Aulrich came to Cat's Cradle to start a new life for himself and found himself joining the late baron in the Salt Wars. When the fighting was over, and with the connections and wealth he acquired, he decided to open a business in the budding town: The Rebellious Boggart Tavern and Game Hall, and business is good. And while he employs a variety of staff (from bartenders to wait staff, entertainers to croupiers, and even his own alchemist team hidden away in the cellar), Aulrich is always looking for trustworthy freelancers to check out the competition throughout town.

At 6th Level: Aulrich finds himself in a bit of a pickle these days. In his attempt at expanding his ownership over various businesses throughout the city of Cat's Cradle, he has inadvertently upset Willowren Skystar, an elven entrepreneur and rival businessperson in town who has strong political ties to nobles in Baron Scale's circles. While there hasn't been any open conflict between Willowren and Aulrich, each has been sending agents to spy on and disrupt each other's interests in Cat's Cradle. Aulrich has reached out to some of the other tavern and inn owners in Old Town and the Gold District (such as the Upper Crust Inn and Treesa's Pub) in an attempt to gain support. As their establishments are streets apart from one another, and not in any direct competition with one another, Aulrich hopes to create an alliance that serves to be mutually beneficial for all involved, while also undermining the enterprises of Ser Skystar.

At 10th Level: Having recently recovered from an assassination attempt on his life, Aulrich is even more gruff and rough in nature but is invigorated more than ever with a new level of determination and gusto for life. Unlike in years past where the tavern owner kept a reasonable distance from the general crowds frequenting his establishment, choosing instead to observe them from his private interior second-story balcony overlooking the entirety of the main floor hall of the tavern, he now sits openly at a game table near the main bar. Aulrich is usually accompanied by one of his lieutenants and a scribe or courier to take and deliver notes, as well as an entertainer of some description. While he keeps his disdain for the current rulership in check to avoid any direct trouble with Baron Scale's men, Aulrich has begun secretly communicating with interested parties in the rival city of Five-and-Copper to the east.

Aulrich Steelspade, Male Dwarf (Ftr3): HP 20; AC 6[13]; **Atk** war hammer (1d4+1) or scimitar (1d6); **Move** 9; **Save** 12; **AL** N; **CL/XP** 3/60; **Special:** darkvision (60ft), detect stonework, multiple attacks (3) vs. creatures with 1 or fewer HD. **Equipment:** ring mail, war hammer, scimitar.

Aulrich Steelspade, Male Dwarf (Ftr6): HP 38; AC 5[14]; **Atk** *+1 war hammer* (1d4+2) or scimitar (1d6); **Move** 9; **Save** 8; **AL** N; **CL/XP** 6/400; **Special:** darkvision (60ft), detect stonework, multiple attacks (3) vs. creatures with 1 or fewer HD. **Equipment:** chainmail, *+1 war hammer*, scimitar.

Aulrich Steelspade, Male Dwarf (Ftr10): HP 55; AC 5[14]; **Atk** *+1 war hammer* (1d4+8) or scimitar (1d6+6); **Move** 9; **Save** 5; **AL** N; **CL/XP** 10/1400; **Special:** darkvision (60ft), detect stonework, multiple attacks (3) vs. creatures with 1 or fewer HD. **Equipment:** chainmail, *+1 war hammer*, scimitar, *gauntlets of ogre power*.

BARON SCALE

A young and inexperienced baron, Scale is only 19 years old. He is an even-tempered and serious young man, yet friendly to everyone regardless of status. While it is clear that most of the running of Cat's Cradle is being handled by Scale's mother and advisers, it is also clear that Scale takes an interest in every subject and takes seriously his duties and responsibilities. He listens to all sides of a matter before approving his advisers' recommendations, seeking to truly understand all sides of an issue before he signs off on their decisions.

At 3rd Level: Because he is working hard to finish his education while participating fully in his baronial duties, Scale is always busy. His advisers book those social events they think will benefit his long-term position as baron, and Scale makes little other room in his schedule for relaxation or entertainment. Those seeking an audience must either convince his advisers that a meeting is worthwhile, wait through the long lines to address him publicly during his twice-a-week all-comers audience hall, get invited to the sorts of parties he must attend for networking purposes, or catch him during a rare quiet moment, such as between his various daily lessons. This last is perhaps the most difficult, as his guards rarely let strangers get close.

At 6th Level: At the age of 27, Baron Scale is handsome, charming, and masterful, easily able to take command of any situation. He is even-tempered and highly energetic, but he keeps himself very busy, making little time for relaxation or entertainment. That said, Scale does make time for networking events with the city's wealthy and higher-class. In charm and bearing he can seem so perfect at times that it is difficult to believe he is real, or that he is merely a baron.

Underneath this perfect veneer, however, Scale shows signs of a cunning intellect and a shrewd skill for manipulation. Indeed, as courteous and charming as he is, the man is also often difficult to read or predict. What is certain is that

Cat's Cradle is prospering under his rule, and the common people like and respect him. The aristocracy and well-to-do seem to find Scale less flawless — far too concerned for their tastes with the plight of the commoner — but so charming and clever they can't quite seem to dislike him either.

Scale is known to possess a serviceable skill with his ancestors' renowned enchanted blade and the ability to deal honestly with those who deal honestly with him. Due to his strict instructions to his advisers, it is easiest to gain an audience with him by using the right key phrases in requesting an appointment. Scale's secretaries will make appointments for well-spoken, respectfully garbed visitors (regardless of social class) if they can make a good case for their visit to the baron being beneficial to all the people of his holdings. Scale is said to have no interest in his own personal gain, though as he is quite a wealthy man, this may be an exaggeration.

At 10th Level: At 36, Baron Scale is a doting husband and father of two small children. His wife, Liera, is the youngest daughter of a distant count, and she and her husband make a highly effective and likeminded pair working together toward their common goals of peace and prosperity for Cat's Cradle. Starting a family seems to have softened Baron Scale, such that he has become easier to read and more honest about his goals.

This has had the effect of making the man more popular than ever with his people, but his moves have also become easier to predict, and his support among the wealthy and upper classes is slipping. It seems clear to these sections of society that Baron Scale cares more for the poor than the rich and has no interest in larger-scale power games.

The baron and his wife, however, remain charming and courteous at those upper-scale events they feel compelled to attend, and the baron is still a cunning long-term strategist and natural leader, able to manipulate even those who dislike him to make the deals Cat's Cradle needs for its long-term prosperity. He dislikes flattery and is well known for his swordplay.

Baron Scale, Male Human Baron (Ftr3): HP 21; AC 4[15]; Atk rapier (1d6+1); **Move** 12; **Save** 12; **AL** L; **CL/XP** 3/60; **Special:** +1 to hit and damage strength bonus.
Equipment: chainmail, shield, rapier, royal seal.
Note: Baron Scale is constantly accompanied by 1d6+2 loyal bodyguards.

Baron Scale, Male Human Baron (Ftr6): HP 39; AC 2[17]; Atk *+2 flaming rapier* (1d6+3 + 1d6 fire); **Move** 12; **Save** 8; **AL** L; **CL/XP** 6/400; **Special:** +1 to hit and damage strength bonus.

Equipment: plate mail, shield, ancestral *+2 flaming rapier*, royal seal.
Note: Baron Scale is constantly accompanied by 1d6+2 loyal bodyguards.

Baron Scale, Male Human Baron (Ftr10): HP 65; AC 0[19]; Atk *+2 flaming rapier* (1d6+3 + 1d6 fire); **Move** 12; **Save** 5; **AL** L; **CL/XP** 10/1400; **Special:** +1 to hit and damage strength bonus.
Equipment: *+2 plate mail*, shield, ancestral *+2 flaming rapier*, royal seal.
Note: Baron Scale is constantly accompanied by 1d6+2 loyal knights.

Bodyguards, Male or Female Humans (1d6+2): HD 1; AC 7[12]; Atk weapon (1d8); **Move** 12; **Save** 17; **AL** Any; **CL/XP** 1/15; **Special:** none. (*Monstrosities* 257)

Knights, Male or Female Humans (1d6+2): HD 3; AC 5[14]; Atk weapon (1d8); **Move** 12; **Save** 14; **AL** Any; **CL/XP** 3/60; **Special:** none. (*Monstrosities* 256)

ERROL SYLVANNIS

A tall, emaciated man with sallow skin pulls his tattered black robes closer around himself as he moves away from the larger crowds. His bright blue eyes are watery and red-ringed but dart around with acute attention, soaking in his surroundings. He uses a four-foot rod made of a single piece of bone to prod at some of the wares of a market stall before scowling in the direction of some passing guards, and hurries away.

At 3rd Level: Errol's life has been filled with tragedy for as long as he can remember. When he was a youth, he and his family were forced to flee their home due to foreign invaders. Those who were not butchered were forced into squalor, living in filthy conditions as place after place turned them away. The family members who survived these harsh times as refugees finally found a new home, but unfortunately soon perished due to sickness. Errol always had a knack for learning new skills and was able to tap into the arcane energies of the universe. He had aspirations to one day join one of the arcane colleges, but these back-to-back horrible events broke the mind of the young lad. He leaned into this magical aptitude, stealing potions and scrolls in an attempt to either turn back time or to return his fallen family to him. As one can imagine, things did not go well for him. Years later, Errol finds himself in Cat's Cradle. The tales of the power of the salts drew him here, and he looks to add them to his ongoing dark and dangerous experiments.

At 6th Level: Skirting around the city limits, Errol knows the patrol patterns of the guards and soldiers who hassle him the most and avoids them. He prefers to enter the city during shift changes or when the guards on duty prefer simple bribes to let him enter rather than wasting time detaining him. Errol's destinations are always the same: Alchemist's Row and the shop of Jall Krukrich of the ratfolk to pick up supplies and components arcane and of a more unsavory nature. Traveling with him are hooded, cloaked, and enchanted skeletons that act as bodyguards, or as distractions should the occasion arise that Errol needs to make a quick getaway!

At 10th Level: Errol is now situated at the Graveyard of Mur, which is outside the city of Cat's Cradle on the way to the Salt Mines (albeit a bit off the beaten track). While he looks like a withered older man (evidence that his necromantic practices have taken a toll on his general appearance), he is still a vigorous young man in his late 20s. He handles all of the gravedigging and groundskeeping work of the property by himself, preferring to work alone. He finds that people either disapprove of his philosophies, are judgmental of his work, or wish to do him harm. Even though he tends to keep them out of sight as much as he is able, Errol is known to have at least a dozen undead with him at all times. He continues his work for immortality and is constantly seeking rare components, tomes, and spellbooks that can assist him in his quest.

Errol Sylvannis, Male Human Necromancer (MU3): HP 9; AC 9[10] or 2[17] (missile) and 4[15] (melee) from *shield* spell; Atk staff (1d6) or dagger (1d4); **Move** 12; **Save** 13; **AL** C; **CL/XP** 3/60; **Special:** +2 save (spells, wands, staffs), drain health (if Errol injures a creature with a spell or dagger, he gains 1d4 hit points), spells (3/1).
Spells: 1st—*charm person, shield, sleep;* 2nd—*phantasmal force.*
Equipment: staff, dagger, *wand of magic missiles* (8 charges), *potion of healing.*

Errol Sylvannis, Male Human Necromancer (MU6): HP 17; **AC** 8[11] or 2[17] (missile) and 4[15] (melee) from *shield* spell; **Atk** staff (1d6) or *+2 dagger* (1d4+2); **Move** 12; **Save** 9 (+1, ring); **AL** C; **CL/XP** 6/400; **Special:** +2 save (spells, wands, staffs), drain health (if Errol injures a creature with a spell or dagger, he gains 1d6 hit points), spells (4/2/2).
Spells: 1st—*charm person, magic missile, shield, sleep;* 2nd—*darkness 15ft radius, phantasmal force;* 3rd—*invisibility, lightning bolt.*
Equipment: staff, *+2 dagger, ring of protection +1, ring of spell storing (animate dead), wand of cold* (18 charges), *potion of extra healing.*
Note: Errol travels with 1d4+2 disguised skeletons at all times.

Errol Sylvannis, Male Human Necromancer (MU10): HP 31; **AC** 7[12] or 2[17] (missile) and 4[15] (melee) from *shield* spell; **Atk** *staff of power* (2d6) or *+2 dagger* (1d4+2); **Move** 12; **Save** 4 (+2, ring); **AL** C; **CL/XP** 10/1400; **Special:** +2 save (spells, wands, staffs), drain health (if Errol injures a creature with a spell or dagger, he gains 1d8 hit points), spells (4/4/3/2/2).
Spells: 1st—*charm person, magic missile, shield, sleep;* 2nd—*darkness 15ft radius, phantasmal force;* 3rd—*invisibility, lightning bolt.*
Equipment: *staff of power* (32 charges), *+2 dagger, ring of protection +2, ring of spell storing (animate dead), potion of extra healing.*
Note: Errol travels with 1d4+2 disguised skeletons at all times.

Skeletons (1d4+2): HD 1; **AC** 8[11] or 7[12] with shield; **Atk** weapon or strike (1d6) or (1d6+1 two-handed); **Move** 12; **Save** 17; **AL** N; **CL/XP** 1/15; **Special:** immune to sleep and charm spells. (*Monstrosities* 428)

FLOYD THE BAKER

The proprietor of the Happy Surprise Bakery in the Gold District of Cat's Cradle is a pleasant, portly man over average height with light chestnut hair that is starting to go gray. He has no facial hair other than bushy, prominent mutton chops down the sides of his face that reach his jawline. Wearing a cook's apron, this human man has a smile on his reddish, ruddy face and a twinkle in his bright green eyes.

At 3rd Level: Floyd Tarryfoot — or Floyd the Baker to everyone in town — is known for his wonderful fresh bread, his "good spirit" pastries (said to have blessings baked right into them!), and for his jovial laugh. While not officially an alchemist or apothecary, he is a cleric and often has a handful of lesser potions for sale in his shop, placed on his immaculate oak countertop right next to the freshly baked cookies. When not inside tending to customers or seeing to his ovens, Floyd sits out on the front stoop of the shop chatting with some of the town locals, a passing guard, or travelers looking for some supplies. He often can be found recounting outlandish tales he has overheard from his customers (either told directly to him or from talking among themselves). While he denies being any source of information or even one to further rumors, he always seems to have something ready to tell as he gives a little nudge and wink.

At 6th Level: After a lengthy renovation period of his shop (which the characters may have been roped into by their friendly neighborhood baker), the Happy Surprise Bakery has reopened and is better than ever! With glass window displays showing off his fresh baked goods, racks of sugars, spices, and potions, and tables both inside and out to have warm drinks, the place is a welcoming haven. Unbeknownst to anyone, Floyd has set up a shrine underneath the shop in devotion to his deity: Loki, the god of mischief and trickery. A devout follower, Floyd has worked for years to master the arts of deception, misinformation, and practical jokes. While he never intentionally performs these duties with malice or harm in his heart, he gets no greater joy than leading someone astray or causing a mishap. Maybe it was a swapped potion label or serving decaf instead of a caffeinated beverage, or maybe that rumor that illegal goods were being shipped in through slip four at midnight was completely up-to-snuff. In any event, Floyd gets a good laugh, and at the end of the day, no one gets hurt.

At 10th Level: At the behest of his patron deity, Floyd has expanded giving misinformation into a side job to his thriving bakery business. Never wanting the trail to ever make his way back to him, Floyd has started forging bounty notices, help wanted posters, lost item requests, and missing persons reports that he has posted all over town. Not only that, but one in four of his potions is now diluted to either last only half the normal length or to only perform half the desired effect. While he continues with the mindset that he doesn't want any serious harm to come to anyone, he always makes sure to sprinkle a little bit of truth into all of his tricks. Floyd knows that he is starting to cross a dangerous line when it comes to his mischief, but he can't help but find it all so terribly funny.

Floyd Tarryfoot, Male Human Baker and Priest of Loki (Clr3): HP 14; AC 4[15]; **Atk** mace (1d6); **Move** 12; **Save** 13; AL C; **CL/XP** 3/60; **Special:** +2 save vs. paralysis and poison, banish undead, spells (2), trickster (1/day, can hide in shadows, 20%).
Spells: 1st—*cure light wounds, protection from evil.*
Equipment: chainmail, shield, mace.

Floyd Tarryfoot, Male Human Baker and Priest of Loki (Clr6): HP 26; AC 4[15]; **Atk** *+1* mace (1d6+1); **Move** 12; **Save** 10; AL C; **CL/XP** 6/400; **Special:** +2 save vs. paralysis and poison, banish undead, spells (2/2/1/1), trickster (1/day, can hide in shadows, 35%).
Spells: 1st—*cure light wounds, protection from evil.*
Equipment: chainmail, shield, *+1* mace.

Floyd Tarryfoot, Male Human Baker and Priest of Loki (Clr10): HP 38; AC 3[16]; **Atk** *staff of striking* (2d6); **Move** 12; **Save** 6; AL C; **CL/XP** 10/1400; **Special:** +2 save vs. paralysis and poison, banish undead, spells (3/3/3/3/3), trickster (1/day, can hide in shadows, 75%).
Spells: 1st—*cure light wounds, detect magic, protection from evil*; 2nd—*hold person, find traps, silence 15ft radius*; 3rd—*cure disease, locate object, speak with dead*; 4th—*cure serious wounds, neutralize poison, sticks to snakes*; 5th—*create food, dispel evil, insect plague.*
Equipment: *+2 chainmail, staff of striking, potion of clairvoyance, potion of extra healing.*

Garron Thorn

Thorn is outwardly an unassuming halfling who dresses modestly and seems relatively ordinary save for the well-used short sword at his side. Though his overall demeanor is calm and can be quite garrulous and even friendly, Thorn is infamous for his fiery temper, which can explode into acts of appalling violence — mercilessly beating victims, engaging in the torture of those who have resisted his gang's protection rackets, and even nailing the limbs and heads of disloyal minions to the floor. Thorn's cruelty has created a cult of fear and respect, as he allows only the most fanatical and loyal of Kennock operatives to join his growing organization.

At 3rd Level: One of the Kennock Syndicate's most trusted operatives in the Ovens District, Garron Thorn is a halfling whose character is made of equal parts ruthlessness and cunning. A rising star with the Syndicate, Thorn leads a crew of 20 or so low-level soldiers who specialize in protection, extortion, and petty robbery. His self-applied nickname "The Boss of Bricktown" has begun to catch on, earning him even more notoriety in the eyes of Old Man Kennock.

At 6th Level: The Boss of Bricktown has fully earned his moniker and now controls a small army of thugs and operatives as one of Old Man Kennock's most trusted subordinates. He dresses in gray and black, and habitually wears a broad-brimmed black hat pulled low over his eyes. He has grown smarter, crueler, and even more clever, but with his successes have come troubles as well. Ensconced in a well-protected home in the heart of the Ovens, Garron Thorn is intensely jealous of his power and increasingly fearful of competition from other aspiring gang leaders. He has also developed a deep fear of the water — a liability in a lake city like Cat's Cradle. He particularly fears the serpents that lurk in the deep water, and a single monster he calls only "Winston" in particular. Some of Thorn's associates feel that he is losing his mind, and that "Winston" is nothing but a figment of his imagination.

At 10th Level: At the height of his power, Thorn is the undisputed gang chief of the Ovens, but his crippling paranoia and fear keeps him in his fortified residence, from which he oversees Syndicate operations, issues orders, disciplines subordinates, and metes out justice to turncoats or uncooperative

shopkeepers. He has avoided arrest by the watch and by those members of the constabulary determined to bring him to justice, yet he grows increasingly fearful, still afraid of the lake and the ever-present "Winston," whom he claims watches him through his windows at night.

Garron Thorn, The Boss of Bricktown, Male Halfling Assassin (Asn3): HP 14; AC 7[12]; **Atk** short sword (1d6 + sleep poison) or light crossbow (1d4+1 + sleep poison); **Move** 9; **Save** 13; AL C; **CL/XP** 3/60; **Special:** backstab (x2), disguise, poison use, thieving skills.
Thieving Skills: Climb 85%, Tasks/Traps 20%, Hear 3 in 6, Hide 20%, Silent 30%, Locks 20%.
Equipment: leather armor, short sword, light crossbow, 10 bolts, vial of sleep poison (save or sleep for 1d4 hours).

Garron Thorn, The Boss of Bricktown, Male Halfling Assassin (Asn6): HP 26; AC 6[13]; **Atk** short sword (1d6 + poison) or light crossbow (1d4+1 + poison); **Move** 9; **Save** 12 (+1, ring); AL C; **CL/XP** 6/400; **Special:** backstab (x3), disguise, poison use, thieving skills.
Thieving Skills: Climb 88%, Tasks/Traps 35%, Hear 4 in 6, Hide 35%, Silent 45%, Locks 35%.
Equipment: *boots of leaping,* leather armor, short sword, light crossbow, 10 bolts, *ring of protection +1,* vial of poison (save or die).

Garron Thorn, The Boss of Bricktown, Male Halfling Assassin (Asn10): HP 41; AC 6[13]; **Atk** *+1 short sword* (1d6+1 + poison) or light crossbow (1d4+1 + poison); **Move** 9; **Save** 5 (+1, ring); AL C; **CL/XP** 10/1400; **Special:** backstab (x4), disguise, poison use, thieving skills.
Thieving Skills: Climb 92%, Tasks/Traps 60%, Hear 5 in 6, Hide 65%, Silent 70%, Locks 65%.
Equipment: *boots of leaping, +1 leather armor, +1 short sword,* light crossbow, 10 bolts, *ring of protection +1, dust of disappearance,* vial of poison (save or die).

Helezia Arren

An accomplished spellcaster in her hometown, Helezia Arren ventured to Cat's Cradle in the hope of learning the trade of alchemy at the city college. Despite her magical accomplishment, the college's fees proved too expensive and forced her to work as a freelance spellcaster and occasional adventurer, as well as serving as an assistant to her instructors in exchange for discounted tuition. She has taken to her classes with enthusiasm, prompting her instructors to describe her as a natural talent. If encountered, she will always be carrying 2d6 randomly determined potions or alchemical substances (see Appendix A).

At 3rd Level: Helezia is quietly obsessed with her science, to the extent that she doesn't pay much attention to her appearance or keeping her garments in order, and presents herself as a somewhat wild-haired, intense-eyed woman clad in modest garments more suited to a country villager than a skilled wizard and aspiring alchemist. Despite her eccentricities — or perhaps because of them — she is popular with adventurers and other transient, knockabout types who appreciate her presence on explorations or dungeon delves, where she is far more interested in collecting rare substances and potions than in gold and other traditional treasures.

At 6th Level: In her third year at the college, Helezia continues to grow and evolve into a skilled alchemist. She earns significant income from sales of her various products, both through Academy Sales and on her own. Her popularity as an adventuring companion has grown as well, and now she is finding her schedule starting to get crowded as she divides her time between class and dungeoneering. Her potions are more potent now, further adding to her popularity.

At 10th Level: On the verge of graduation, Helezia has been the head of the Alchemical Students' Organization for a year now and contemplates taking employment as a part-time instructor at the college. Though she still occasionally ventures out of Cat's Cradle with adventurers, she more frequently employs them herself, sending them out to obtain rare and important ingredients.

Helezia Arren, Female Human Magic-User (MU3): HP 6; AC 9[10] or 2[17] (missile) and 4[15] (melee) from *shield* spell; **Atk** staff (1d6); **Move** 12; **Save** 13; **AL** L; **CL/XP** 3/60; **Special:** +2 save (spells, wands, staffs), spells (3/1).

Spells: 1st—*charm person, magic missile, shield*; 2nd—*light*.
Equipment: robes, staff, *wand of magic missiles* (12 charges), *potion of clairaudience, potion of healing, potion of fire resistance, potion of treasure finding.*

Helezia Arren, Female Human Magic-User (MU6): HP 14; AC 8[11] or 2[17] (missile) and 4[15] (melee) from *shield* spell; **Atk** *+1 staff* (1d6+1); **Move** 12; **Save** 9 (+1, cloak); **AL** L; **CL/XP** 6/400; **Special:** +2 save (spells, wands, staffs), spells (4/2/2).
Spells: 1st—*charm person, magic missile, read magic, shield*; 2nd—*light, phantasmal force*; 3rd—*dispel magic, hold person.*
Equipment: robes, *+1 staff, cloak of protection +1, wand of cold* (15 charges), *beaker of potions, potion of flying, potion of invisibility, potion of fire resistance.*

Helezia Arren, Female Human Magic-User (MU10): HP 24; AC 8[11] or 2[17] (missile) and 4[15] (melee) from *shield* spell; **Atk** *staff of wizardry* (2d6); **Move** 12; **Save** 5 (+1, cloak); **AL** L; **CL/XP** 10/1400; **Special:** +2 save (spells, wands, staffs), spells (4/4/3/2/2).
Spells: 1st—*charm person, magic missile, read magic, shield*; 2nd—*light, locate object, phantasmal force, wizard lock*; 3rd—*dispel magic, hold person, lightning bolt*; 4th—*dimension door, remove curse*; 5th—*hold monster, teleport.*
Equipment: robes, *staff of wizardry* (42 charges), *cloak of protection +1, ring of fire resistance, beaker of potions, potion of extra healing, potion of invulnerability,* scroll (*confusion, wizard eye*).

Henric Hammerhill

A stout dwarven man with dark skin and a long black beard that he keeps braided and clasped to his studded leather jerkin. His shaven head is kept covered with his hooded cloak and a leather cap inscribed with the pattern of a bird of prey. While seemingly like any other dwarf at first glance, he is surprisingly more agile and stealthy than his slower-moving, stocky brethren. When springing into combat, he either uses a short sword or hand axe, fires his elaborately engraved shortbow, or swings his mithril-headed war hammer.

At 3rd Level: Relatively new to Cat's Cradle, Henric Hammerhill came into the region from the west riding a dwarven war ram and accompanied by his only friend and companion: a black-and-red feathered axe beak by the name of Muuaji. Without a silver to his name, he has begun hiring his services out to the locals in exchange for coin when he can get it (or food, drink, and lodging when he cannot). While not yet familiar with the surrounding terrain, Henric is a skilled survivalist and hunter who has begun to earn the reputation of being reliable and honest, keeping a level head in tense situations and being a voice of reason. Whether it be helping track something in the wilds, provide an extra blade in battle, or guarding people along the trade routes in and out of town, the stoic Henric Hammerhill is willing to do just about anything within his skill set for pay.

At 6th Level: One of the prominent hunters and trackers in the region, Henric Hammerhill can usually be found sitting quietly on the porch of one of the better known taverns or inns in town. Accompanying him nearby (or sometimes even at his table, making a mess and eating bits of leftover venison) is his axe beak companion Muuaji. Both dwarf and large bird watch passersby with a modicum of interest, content in their solitude but ready for any job should the opportunity present itself. Henric often provides guidance to those new to the area and who need to get their bearing when traversing the surrounding wilderness, but also provides game to the local food merchants (sanctioned by the city lords, of course).

As most of his time is dedicated toward official hunting trips or for performing escort missions, Henric is always in need of people to handle a few odd jobs for him. He may require a package of meat to be delivered to an out-of-the-way client or perhaps to pick up a bundle of expensive hides from a furrier who has had some bandit trouble of late. On a more personal note, Hammerhill is looking for someone who can track down and handle a tribe of goblins in the nearby forest who have been rumored to be training owlbears to aid in their harassment of other rangers, woodsmen, and even miners in the region.

At 10th Level: Henric Hammerhill has become a bit of a recluse during the course of the last few years. While still known as one of the premiere hunters and trackers of the region, he no longer attends the court nor offers his services to anyone since the deaths of his family at the hands (or more accurately, claws and fangs) of Jokulvargr, an awakened

demonic winter wolf. Henric has all but retired, keeping to himself at his cabin in the woods outside of Cat's Cradle, still accompanied by his axe beak Muuaji. In actuality though, Henric seeks out knowledge and allies in order to one day mount an expedition to the extradimensional home plane where Jokulvargr resides, along with her pack known as the Burning Frost Tribe. Information, equipment, and magic for planar travel is what Henric now seeks to obtain, and he will pay handsomely for any brought to him.

Henric Hammerhill, Male Dwarf Ranger (Rgr3): HP 26; **AC** 7[12]; **Atk** hand axe (1d6) or war hammer (1d4+1) or shortbow x2 (1d6); **Move** 9; **Save** 12; **AL** L; **CL/XP** 3/60; **Special:** +3 damage vs. giants and goblin-types, alertness, tracking. **Equipment:** leather armor, hand axe, war hammer, shortbow, 20 arrows, animal companion (Muuaji).

Henric Hammerhill, Male Dwarf Ranger (Rgr6): HP 43; **AC** 4[15]; **Atk** hand axe (1d6+8) or *+1 war hammer* (1d4+10) or shortbow x2 (1d6); **Move** 9; **Save** 9; **AL** L; **CL/XP** 6/400; **Special:** +6 damage vs. giants and goblin-types, alertness, tracking. **Equipment:** *bracers of defense AC 4[15], girdle of giant strength,* hand axe, *+1 war hammer,* shortbow, 20 arrows, animal companion (Muuaji).

Henric Hammerhill, Male Dwarf Ranger (Rgr10): HP 61; **AC** 4[15]; **Atk** *+2 flaming hand axe* (1d6+10 + 1d6 fire) or *+1 war hammer* (1d4+10) or shortbow x2 (1d6); **Move** 9; **Save** 5; **AL** L; **CL/XP** 10/1400; **Special:** +10 damage vs. giants and goblin-types, alertness, tracking. **Equipment:** *bracers of defense AC 4[15], girdle of giant strength,* +2 hand axe, *+1 war hammer,* shortbow, 20 arrows, animal companion (Muuaji).

Muuaji, Axe Beak: HD 3; **HP** 19; **AC** 5[14]; **Atk** 2 claws (1d6) and bite (2d6); **Move** 18; **Save** 14; **AL** N; **CL/XP** 3/60; **Special:** none. (***The Tome of Horrors Complete*** 621)

Jall Kukrich

Though his wiry body is taller by about six inches, Jall Kukrich's hunched stature marks him as just over four-foot-six. He does his best to keep his black and gray fur clean by washing from unoccupied watering troughs, and he keeps his facial fur and whiskers slicked back with a bit of wagon wheel axle grease he keeps in a tiny glass jar. He wears an odd, ill-fitting outfit that consists of an old nobleman's long cape sewn together with a discarded entertainer's outfit and some clergyman's robes. Atop his head he wears his most prized possession: an immaculate crushed velvet red fez, complete with black-and-gold threaded tassel. Unlike the rest of his attire, his headpiece is always clean and sits at such a perfect angle that passersby cannot help but smile at Jall when they see him wearing it.

At 3rd Level: Like most ratfolk in the Lost Lands, Jall has been a bit of an outcast within the city since his early days. Arriving by river on a raft made of sticks and muck, he began working odd jobs at the docks, everything from assisting fishermen to moving crates and barrels to standing guard at warehouses. But while he worked hard, he was really keeping his ear to the ground, learning what he could about the city and its residents: whispers, rumors, stories, deals, schedules; any bit of information he could turn around and tell interested parties for a bit of coin. Jall has befriended the young street urchins and unnoticed youths of the city to help him learn more and from farther out, creating a loose information network throughout the Docks, Old Town, and the Ovens. He himself is also looking for any kind of odd job that can either earn him a bit of coin or something of value (assuming he is not risking his life or anything else dangerous like that!)

At 6th Level: You can usually hear the bell tinkling on the covered two-wheeled cart Jall pulls behind him before you see his fez-adorned smiling rodent face. He moves his moderately sized "establishment" throughout the Docks, Old Town, the Ovens, and even the southern and eastern areas of the Gold District, calling out to new travelers and adventurers he sees or to citizens he has come to know over the years. Jall's mobile shop sells a variety of goods and items, and he is always looking to make a trade, even if he has to offer a discount. However, information is what he deals with more: Do you need dirt on what the corrupt guardsman Sergeant Donovon is handling these days? Or what time a Gold District shopkeep locks up shop and goes home for the night? Perhaps you are wanting to know the latest rumors of the gemstone vein discovered in one of the Salt Mines? These types of things are what Jall excels at knowing and selling, as his network of little spies and information-gatherers has grown exponentially. He now has information from all over the city of Cat's Cradle and the surrounding area, even from as far as the village of Gambit. However, information has a price, and while gold is always nice, offering up substantiated intel on something Jall doesn't know is preferred.

At 10th Level: Situated in the southern area of the Gold District, close to Old Town, Jall owns and runs a small bazaar shop he calls The Memorable Fez where he continues to sell a variety of items of all sorts. In addition to maintaining an information network acquired from the cities' underclass youths, Jall has branched out into employing pickpockets, burglars, and forgers. Besides providing requested information, he now also offers documents, disguises and uniforms, and even official crests and badges (given the appropriate amount of time and money). As always, Jall is not a violent creature by nature, but he is willing to pay top dollar to anyone willing to acquire the things he needs, by any means necessary. Having come a long way from being the damp rat standing on a pier in the Docks, he will do anything to keep what he has built up all these years (including working with the city guard and officials if need be). He pays a contribution to the city guards' "retirement fund" every other week to receive information and for them to keep out of his affairs. In addition, he donates a weekly "tithe" to the temple of Freya to stay in their good graces as well, even though he doesn't put any stock into the gods. While Jall asserts that he is a master of his own fate, he still appreciates a good blessing or healing from clerics when in need!

Jall Kukrich, Ratling: HD 2; **HP** 11; **AC** 7[12]; **Atk** bite (1d6 + disease) or scimitar (1d6) or light crossbow (1d4+1); **Save** 16; **Move** 12; **AL** N; **CL/XP** 3/60; **Special:** diseased bite. (*Monstrosities* 388)
Equipment: leather armor, scimitar, light crossbow, 10 bolts, *charming fez* (see sidebar)

Jall Kukrich, Ratling: HD 5; **HP** 28; **AC** 7[12]; **Atk** bite (1d6 + disease) or scimitar (1d6) or light crossbow (1d4+1); **Save** 12; **Move** 12; **AL** N; **CL/XP** 6/400; **Special:** diseased bite. (*Monstrosities* 388)
Equipment: leather armor, scimitar, light crossbow, 10 bolts, *charming fez* (see sidebar)

Jall Kukrich, Ratling: HD 9; **HP** 49; **AC** 7[12]; **Atk** bite (1d6 + disease) or scimitar (1d6) or light crossbow (1d4+1); **Save** 6; **Move** 12; **AL** N; **CL/XP** 10/1400; **Special:** diseased bite. (*Monstrosities* 388)
Equipment: leather armor, scimitar, light crossbow, 10 bolts, *charming fez* (see sidebar)

KAMARA B'DU

This tall, striking woman with ebony skin cannot help but have a confident, regal stance, despite her obvious attempts to blend in with the crowd. The armor she wears is accented in white and blue with gold edging and has clearly been perfectly crafted specifically for her. Although she tries to assume a demure attitude, her warm golden brown eyes flash with a confidence and self-assuredness that is unmatched.

At 3rd Level: Kamara B'du was born during a convergence of environmental anomalies: It was on a night where no stars were seen in the sky, but instead there were two full moons. And just as dawn broke, a meteor shower began, the shooting stars dissipating as the sun's morning light welcomed in the birth of little Kamara. All her life she heard that she was destined for greatness, to lead the people to the promised land, to bring the waters of life to the barren deserts, to make the world great again like it was in the Age of Heroes. Kamara grew to hate words such as "prophecy" and "destiny," wishing only to help those in need. She cared nothing for praise or recognition, and knew that the only way she would escape from all the attention would be to leave her homeland and travel to a place where no one knew who she was.

While a healer isn't exactly what is needed right now in Cat's Cradle, Kamara still finds herself needed for other divine services, providing knowledge and guidance to any that come for her. Still wishing not to gain any level of notoriety, she rarely works out of any of the popular churches or religious gathering locations, instead opting to work privately in caravan camps or out of taverns and inns. Aside from her expertise in medicines and healing, it is her knowledge in the divine and history that are most often sought after by those looking for guidance.

At 6th Level: Recently struck by a series of dreams with imagery of celestial entities combatting an unknown darkness, with her as a pivotal figure fighting on the side of light, Kamara has had her opinion of destiny challenged. Because of this, Kamara has reluctantly started a small religious faction dedicated to magic, healing, and shining a cleansing light into the dark corners of the world. Plagued now by the bureaucracy of the city and the corruption that comes from within, Kamara is in constant need of assistance in protecting her temple and her followers who ask for aid and guidance when others turn them away.

At 10th Level: After all these years, Kamara B'du has decided to embrace her destiny. After a powerful encounter with an angel, a deva named Zephiriel,

the hidden potential within her was tapped and Kamara's celestial heritage blossomed. She is still coming to grips with what that means about her dreams and visions, but her confidence in herself and her new path are clear. She hopes to get a message back to her family to let them all know what has happened, with her returning to them one day.

Kamara's order, now calling themselves the Guardians of the Light, have around 30 primary members and double that in acolytes. The ranked regular primaries consist of clerics, paladins, fighters, and alchemists dedicated to helping those in need, seeking the truth in all things, and fighting evil whenever they can. While services are held every dawn by her cleric underlings, Kamara leads sermons only for special occasions, holidays, and on the evenings of a full moon.

The Guardians of Light have grown too big for their previous headquarters and are seeking a larger locale. They pay characters a "finder's fee" for information on a suitable location (either within the city of Cat's Cradle or in the surrounding land) to which they can relocate.

Kamara B'du, Female Human Priestess (Clr3): HP 14; AC 5[14]; **Atk** mace (1d6); **Move** 12; **Save** 14; **AL** L; **CL/XP** 3/60; **Special:** +2 save vs. paralysis and poison, banish undead, spells (2).
Spells: 1st—*cure light wounds*.
Equipment: ring mail, shield, mace.

Kamara B'du, Female Human Priestess (Clr6): HP 29; AC 4[15]; **Atk** *+1 mace* (1d6); **Move** 12; **Save** 10; **AL** L; **CL/XP** 6/400; **Special:** +2 save vs. paralysis and poison, banish undead, divine strike (1/day, additional 1d6 damage), spells (2/2/1/1).
Spells: 1st—*cure light wounds, purify food and drink*; 2nd—*bless, hold person*; 3rd—*cure disease*; 4th—*cure serious wounds*.
Equipment: chainmail, shield, *+1 mace*.

Kamara B'du, Female Human Priestess of the Guardians of Light (Clr10): HP 39; AC 2[17]; **Atk** *+2 mace that destroys undead* (1d6+2); **Move** 12; **Save** 6; **AL** L; **CL/XP** 10/1400; **Special:** +2 save vs. paralysis and poison, banish undead, divine strike (3/day, additional 1d6 damage), magic resistance (10%), spells (3/3/3/3/3).
Spells: 1st—*cure light wounds, detect evil, purify food and drink*; 2nd—*bless, hold person, speak with animals*; 3rd—*cure disease, prayer, speak with dead*; 4th—*create water, cure serious wounds, neutralize poison*; 5th—*commune, create food, raise dead*.
Equipment: *+1 fiery plate mail*, shield, *+2 mace that destroys undead*, 2 potions of extra healing.

Mattea Theasean

Young and devoted to keeping order in Cat's Cradle, Mattea Theasean joined the city watch several years ago, quickly rising through the ranks while growing disillusioned with the organization's corruption and lax attitude toward law enforcement. When she was involved in tracking down the Dockside Lurker, a ruthless robber and murderer who plagued the waterfront, Mattea gained the notice of Lady Genera, the tough and wizened commander of the constabulary and was recruited into the organization. Mattea immediately distinguished herself and, when uprooting a smuggling operation by the Kennock Syndicate, proved to be utterly incorruptible. In the process, she made several prominent enemies but continued to perform her duty, completely undeterred.

At 3rd Level: Over the years, Mattea has studied arcane and divine magic, applying it to her career as an investigator. She cuts a dramatic figure, clad in her long leather coat, armed with a rapier and a hand crossbow with poisoned bolts. Her spellcasting abilities and her choice of weapons has led some to suggest that she has some history with the drow, or may indeed have dark elf ancestors, but Mattea herself is quite secretive about her past.

At 6th Level: Despite years on the street and continued exposure to even more corruption and crime, Mattea has grown more compassionate toward victims and has even begun to develop a certain understanding and empathy for some criminals, seeing that some folk are forced into lives of illegal activities by circumstances beyond their control. One sign of her evolving nature is her professional alliance with private investigator Valdrin Hoff, an individual known for his hatred of crime that victimizes the weak and his tendency to mete out justice on his own terms. Though she feels some distaste for Hoff's occasional vigilantism, she nevertheless continues to share information with him, though she has kept their relationship quiet, especially to her superiors.

She carries a scar on her face from a Syndicate assassin, and she refuses any

arcane healing or cosmetic surgery. Her signature leather coat is enchanted, and she carries the unique *investigator's staff* and is accompanied by her raven familiar, Kaen.

At 10th Level: Now a senior investigator and thought by many to one day be destined for the office of Chief Constable, Mattea Theasean has grown into a far more compassionate and pragmatic individual than she was earlier in her career. Though she is scarred, tough, and uncompromising in her pursuit of criminals, she has learned much about forgiveness and understanding. While others who enforce the law may have become more cynical and grim-hearted, Theasean appears to have gone in the other direction, and today is a dedicated defender of the weak and the downtrodden, willing to overlook or lend help to those whom circumstances force into illegal acts. Crime bosses, killers, career criminals and others should not rely on her merciful streak, however, for she also knows the difference between the unlucky, the ignorant and the truly evil. She continues to wield her trusty *investigator's staff* and a *+2 rapier*, a gift from her grateful fellow constables.

Mattea Theasean, Female Elf City Watch Investigator (Ftr3/MU3/Clr3): HP 12; AC 9[10] or 2[17] (missile) and 4[15] (melee) from *shield* spell; **Atk** rapier (1d6) or light crossbow (1d4+1); **Move** 12; **Save** 12/13/13; **AL** N; **CL/XP** 3/60; **Special:** +2 save (spells, wands, staffs), darkvision (60ft), detect secret doors, immune to paralysis, spells (MU 3/1, Clr 2).
Spells: 1st—*cure light wounds, detect magic, light, magic missile, shield*; 2nd—*invisibility*.
Equipment: rapier, light crossbow, 10 bolts.

Mattea Theasean, Female Elf City Watch Investigator (Ftr6/MU6/Clr6): HP 22; AC 8[11] or 2[17] (missile) and 4[15] (melee) from *shield* spell; **Atk** *investigator's staff* (1d6+1) or rapier (1d6) or light crossbow (1d4+1); **Move** 12; **Save** 8/9/9 (+1, ring); **AL** N; **CL/XP** 6/400; **Special:** +2 save (spells, wands, staffs), darkvision (60ft), detect secret doors, immune to paralysis, spells (MU 4/2/2, Clr 2/2/1/1).
Spells: 1st—*cure light wounds, charm person, detect magic, light, magic missile, shield*; 2nd—*bless, find traps, invisibility, phantasmal force*; 3rd—*cure disease, dispel magic, hold person*;

4th—*cure serious wounds*.
Equipment: *investigator's staff* (120 charges) (see sidebar), rapier, light crossbow, 10 bolts, *ring of protection +1*.

Mattea Theasean, Female Elf City Watch Senior Investigator (Ftr10/MU10/Clr10): HP 33; AC 7[12] or 2[17] (missile) and 4[15] (melee) from *shield* spell; **Atk** *investigator's staff* (1d6+1) or *+2 rapier* (1d6+2) or light crossbow (1d4+1); **Move** 12; **Save** 3/4/4 (+2, ring); **AL** N; **CL/XP** 10/1400; **Special:** +2 save (spells, wands, staffs), darkvision (60ft), detect secret doors, immune to paralysis, spells (MU 4/4/3/2/2, Clr 3/3/3/3/3). **Spells:** 1st—*cure light wounds* (x2), *charm person, detect magic, light, magic missile, shield*; 2nd—*bless, detect evil, find traps, invisibility, phantasmal force, speak with animals, web*; 3rd—*cure disease, dispel magic, hold person, lightning bolt, prayer, speak with dead*; 4th—*charm monster, create water, cure serious wounds, dimension door, speak with plants*; 5th—*commune, contact other plane, passwall, quest, raise dead*.
Equipment: *investigator's staff* (61 charges) (see sidebar), *+2 rapier*, light crossbow, 10 bolts, *ring of protection +2*.

Kaen, Raven Familiar: HP 3; AC 6[13]; **Atk** bite (1d2); **Move** 2 (fly 12); **Save** 18; **AL** N; **CL/XP** A/5; **Special:** none. (*Monstrosities* 387)

MINTRA KOHLER

A very pale woman stands unassumingly off to one side, quietly watching her surroundings. While very tall and lanky, she is clearly very fit and athletic. She wears a loose-fitting pair of dark pants and keeps her black-and-white hair pulled up high on the back of her head, held in place by two ornately carved hairpins. She carries a simple drawstring bag on her back and leans against a long quarterstaff made of blackened ironwood. But it is her cold, emotionless black eyes, when she turns her attention to you, that are the most off-putting, especially since her expressionless face does nothing to ease the unnerving tension caused by her stare.

At 3rd Level: When Mintra was just a girl growing up in the Skyforge of the Blue Soul Monastery far to the east, she was part of a small group of youths that experienced a deadly malady. This sickness caused them all to fall into a deep sleep and caused the blood in their veins to harden, almost as hard as stone. Half of the young ones died as a result, but those that recovered and awakened spoke of a shadowy, fog-filled wood and a dark voice calling out to them. As the years passed, each of the children affected by the "Stone Blood Curse" had their memories of the incident washed away, suppressed deep into the recesses of their mind … but not Mintra. Every night since reawakening, she has dreamed of that voice in the dark forest calling out to her, and while it frightened her, she felt drawn to it and compelled to seek it out. When Mintra came of age, she left the monastery to search for answers and to gain knowledge of how to fill the hole she felt in her soul.

At 6th Level: Still new to the Cat's Cradle region, Mintra the monk has struggled to find her place. A region of progress with its bustling commerce and daily turnaround of travelers both to and from the city itself, she quickly realized that the answers she was seeking would not come easily. But she knows she is in the right place, for the world seems more in focus for her than ever before since leaving the Skyforge of the Blue Soul Monastery. Not only that, but the voice from her dreams is now clearer than ever before, its dark song filling her with purpose and calling to her from the wilderness beyond the city walls. Not from the lakes, nor the hills and salt mines, but from the forest; that is where the power has been pulling at her mind. In addition, a name has come to her that she cannot shake: The Shrouded Ruins of Atenam. Whether this name came to her in her sleep, or if she gleaned it off a strange wayfaring traveler, she cannot say, but as soon as she heard it, it was as if a gong had struck within her heart and her head. She knew that if she found this place, her

questions would finally be answered.

At 10th Level: Mintra the Unburnt is the guardian of the hidden Atenam Grove in the Cantricle Forest, acting as a bodyguard and scout, but also as a thug enforcer and kidnapper for her new masters. Freshly imbued with a fiendish blessing by an Archdruid of the Order of the Old Oak for loyalty and services rendered, she has started down the path to become one with the entity that reached out to her all those years ago. While Mintra herself is not a cleric or druid, she has used the energies granted to her to finely hone her martial prowess and to further perfect her body and mind. Often roaming the streets of Cat's Cradle, or frequenting popular taverns within the city, she likes to keep tabs on newcomers into the area or for potential marks she can knock out and take back to the druids of the wood. While she is more than capable of handling herself in a fight, she always has a small squad of young druid acolytes and cutthroats with her, awaiting her signal. Recently, Mintra has been laying low as she recently kidnapped Willowren Skystar, the daughter of a local noble, and smuggled her into the forest.

Mintra Kohler, Female Human Monk (Mnk3): HP 9; AC 7[12]; **Atk** strike (1d6) or light crossbow (1d4+1); **Move** 14; **Save** 13; **AL** N; **CL/XP** 3/60; **Special:** +1 damage with weapons, +2 save vs. paralysis and poison, alertness, deadly strike, deflect missiles, thieving skills.
Thieving Skills: Climb 87%, Tasks/Traps 25%, Hear 4 in 6, Hide 20%, Silent 30%, Locks 20%.
Equipment: light crossbow, 10 bolts.

Mintra Kohler, Female Human Monk (Mnk6): HP 17; AC 4[15]; **Atk** 2 strikes (1d12) or light crossbow (1d4+1); **Move** 17; **Save** 10; **AL** N; **CL/XP** 6/400; **Special:** +2 save vs. paralysis and poison, +3 damage with weapons, alertness, deadly strike, deflect missiles, mastery of mind (resist mind reading 90%), multiple attacks (x2), slow falling (20ft), speak with animals, thieving skills.
Thieving Skills: Climb 90%, Tasks/Traps 40%, Hear 4 in 6, Hide 35%, Silent 45%, Locks 35%.
Equipment: light crossbow, 10 bolts.

Mintra Kohler, the Unburnt, Guardian of the Atenam Grove, Female Human Monk (Mnk10): HP 26; AC 1[18]; **Atk** 2 strikes (2d8+4) or light crossbow (1d4+1); **Move** 21;

Save 6; **AL** N; **CL/XP** 10/1400; **Special:** +2 save vs. paralysis and poison, +5 damage with weapons, alertness, deadly strike, deflect missiles, heal self (1/day, 1d6+4 hp), immune to *geas* and *quest* spells, immune to mind control, mastery of mind (resist mind reading 94%), multiple attacks (x2), slow falling (40ft), speak with animals, thieving skills.
Thieving Skills: Climb 94%, Tasks/Traps 70%, Hear 5 in 6, Hide 75%, Silent 80%, Locks 75%.
Equipment: light crossbow, 10 bolts.

Oja Korbis

This nimble half-elven woman smirks at you from the rafters before falling backward into a double somersault and lands effortlessly on her feet. Wearing leather armor, loose attire, and a belt of knives around her waist, this olive-skinned woman ties a blue sash around her head to keep her flowing black hair out of her eyes before giving another sly smile. "Wotcher!" She flips a pair of daggers out of their sheaths, inspects the blades, then returns them with a spinning flourish.

At 3rd Level: An orphan and runaway, Oja has always been tough and independent, but despite the hardships of her youth, she has never let her positive attitude be diminished. Able to make friends wherever she has traveled, Oja is bold and outgoing, and never backs down from opposition. As she tends to have an affinity with the downtrodden, poor, and "the little guy," Oja has been known to partake in heists or jobs against wealthy targets that she can then turn around and generously give back to those in need.

Although she has only been in Cat's Cradle a short while, Oja has quickly learned who to trust and who to avoid in town, and can serve as a guide for other newcomers. She helps gather information for Jall Kukrich, has a passing friendship with Valdrin Hoff, and is an acquaintance with Garron Thorn (with whom she respectfully keeps out of his business, despite having "acquired" a few items for him when she first arrived in town).

At 6th Level: Oja Korbis, under the guise of the masked vigilante known as the Blue Fox, has made a name for herself by stealing from the rich and powerful to provide support for the orphanages, street urchins, and other poor folk in Cat's Cradle and surrounding locales. While "on the job," Oja tends to work alone, but she still maintains her contacts with the other prominent information brokers and thieves in town as well as making sure she doesn't

step on any toes. She has a more strained relationship with the authorities of town, as her activities have gotten more illegal of late.

Through her various heists, Oja has begun to hone her knowledges and has become a bit of an amateur historian when it comes to pieces of art, rare components, and magic items. She usually fences her items through Jall Kukrich, although lately she has been acquiring some otherworldly pieces of art that she has decided to keep to herself to investigate more. Should any players wish to assist her in her investigations, or should they come across any such items themselves, Oja offers compensation for them.

At 10th Level: Oja Korbis has recently broken her way out of the Cat's Cradle jail with the help of a handful of orphans and street urchins, and is on the lam. Luckily, her persona as the Blue Fox was not compromised, so she is able to operate in disguise as she investigates who betrayed her and framed her for the murder of an alchemist within the city limits (a halfling fellow by the name of Adric Waterhouse). Oja suspects her framing has something to do with the mysterious statuettes and trinkets she has been finding circulating around town. These items give her a growing concern that a dark organization or guild is gathering and starting to operate in the area. Does this have something to do with the mining and salts of the region? Or is there something more sinister afoot? The Blue Fox does not know but hopes she can uncover what is really happening.

Oja Korbis, the Blue Fox, Female Half-Elf Thief (Thf3): HP 7; **AC** 7[12]; **Atk** rapier (1d6) or dagger (1d4) or whip (1d4) or shortbow x2 (1d6); **Move** 12; **Save** 13; **AL** N; **CL/XP** 3/60; **Special:** +2 save bonus vs. traps and magical devices, backstab (x2), darkvision (60ft), read languages, thieving skills.
Thieving Skills: Climb 87%, Tasks/Traps 25%, Hear 4 in 6, Hide 20%, Silent 30%, Locks 20%.
Equipment: rapier, 2 daggers, whip, shortbow, 20 arrows.

Oja Korbis, the Blue Fox, Female Half-Elf Thief (Thf6): HP 15; **AC** 7[12]; **Atk** *+1 rapier* (1d6+1) or dagger (1d4) or whip (1d4) or shortbow x2 (1d6); **Move** 12; **Save** 10; **AL** N; **CL/XP** 6/400; **Special:** +2 save bonus vs. traps and magical devices, backstab (x3), darkvision (60ft), read languages, thieving skills.
Thieving Skills: Climb 90%, Tasks/Traps 40%, Hear 4 in 6, Hide 35%, Silent 45%, Locks 35%.
Equipment: *+1 rapier*, 2 daggers, whip, shortbow, 20 arrows.

Oja Korbis, the Blue Fox, Female Half-Elf Thief (Thf10): HP 25; **AC** 2[17]; **Atk** *+1 rapier* (1d6+1) or dagger (1d4) or whip (1d4) or shortbow x2 (1d6); **Move** 12; **Save** 6; **AL** N; **CL/XP** 10/1400; **Special:** +2 save bonus vs. traps and magical devices, backstab (x4), darkvision (60ft), read languages, thieving skills.
Thieving Skills: Climb 90%, Tasks/Traps 40%, Hear 4 in 6, Hide 35%, Silent 45%, Locks 35%.
Equipment: *bracers of defense AC 4[15], cloak of displacement, +1 rapier*, 2 daggers, whip, shortbow, 20 arrows, *potion of frozen concoction, potion of slipperiness.*

The Raven

The rogue simply known as "The Raven" lurks silently in the shadows, almost becoming one with the darkness. The figure wears a plague doctor style black leather mask that obscures facial features. The lithe, muscular form is dressed in masterfully crafted black-and-silver leather armor and wears a wide-brim hat and cloak. Adorned with countless throwing blades, the rogue also uses a scimitar in melee combat, and a longbow and quiver of black-fletched arrows hangs off the back.

At 3rd Level: This leather-clad elf with blonde and pink hair and a scarred face typically keeps to themselves in the corner of the tavern, drinking their bitter tea and munching on dried fruit. If offered food or drink more delicious than what they are currently imbibing, the Raven declines in a quiet voice, just above a whisper, stating that they don't have a taste for such things. In any case, the lithe rogue doesn't balk at company, nor overtly shy away from direct conversation, despite looking uncomfortable at direct contact with people. Originally from the town of Dancer, the Raven came to Cat's Cradle looking for work and also to find a couple of cousins who came to the region and then went missing.

At 6th Level: Since they received their answers as to the fate of their lost kin, the Raven is now a full-fledged mercenary-for-hire within the city and surrounding areas of Cat's Cradle. Almost exclusively wearing the trademark plague doctor mask wherever they go, the Raven has earned the reputation of someone who gets the job done. Whatever skills are

The Raven, Human Thief (Thf3): HP 10; AC 7[12]; **Atk** scimitar (1d6) or dagger (1d4) or longbow x2 (1d6); **Move** 12; **Save** 13; **AL** N; **CL/XP** 3/60; **Special:** +2 save bonus vs. traps and magical devices, backstab (x2), read languages, thieving skills.
Thieving Skills: Climb 87%, Tasks/Traps 25%, Hear 4 in 6, Hide 20%, Silent 30%, Locks 20%.
Equipment: leather armor, plague doctor mask, scimitar, dagger, longbow, 20 arrows.

The Raven, Human Thief (Ftr1/Thf5): HP 23; AC 5[14]; **Atk** scimitar (1d6) or dagger (1d4) or longbow x2 (1d6); **Move** 12; **Save** 14/11; **AL** N; **CL/XP** 6/400; **Special:** −1[+1] dexterity AC bonus, +1 to hit missile bonus, +2 save bonus vs. traps and magical devices, backstab (x3), read languages, thieving skills.
Thieving Skills: Climb 87%, Tasks/Traps 25%, Hear 4 in 6, Hide 20%, Silent 30%, Locks 20%.
Equipment: +1 leather armor, plague doctor mask, scimitar, dagger, longbow, 20 arrows.

The Raven, Human Thief (Ftr5/Thf5): HP 40; AC 5[14]; **Atk** scimitar (1d6) or dagger (1d4) or longbow x2 (1d6); **Move** 12; **Save** 10/11; **AL** N; **CL/XP** 10/1400; **Special:** −1[+1] dexterity AC bonus, +1 to hit missile bonus, +2 save bonus vs. traps and magical devices, backstab (x3), read languages, thieving skills.
Thieving Skills: Climb 87%, Tasks/Traps 25%, Hear 4 in 6, Hide 20%, Silent 30%, Locks 20%.
Equipment: +1 leather armor, boots of leaping, plague doctor mask, scimitar, dagger, longbow, 20 arrows.

RY'KYNA OF THE GRAY WOLVES

This muscular human woman is clearly a barbarian because of her hide armor, fur coverings, and dark red woad painted upon her. Over her form-fitted leather cuirass, she wears a sleeveless short half-tabard and a large gray wolf pelt cloak over her shoulders. Atop her head, covering her braided fair hair, is the metal open-faced helm of a knight she slew in single combat.

At 3rd Level: Ry'kyna of the Gray Wolves is the third daughter (and ninth overall child) of the human Chieftess Shieldmaiden Tulris One-Eye and her half-orc husband Graystripe of the mighty Gray Wolf tribe from the Razorback Plains on the far side of the Cantricle Forest. The Gray Wolves are a nomadic clan, and while they are more of a baric nature, they actually deal in trade with the pelts and fur they acquire, as well as bone scrimshaw and pieces of arms and armor they take from their fallen enemies. Ry'kyna is loyal to her family and to her tribe, and she is content living the life of a warrior. Like the rest of her family, Ry'kyna is notorious for her blind rage on the battlefield, where she swings her single-bladed, two-handed axe with skill and fury. She is never seen without a weapon nearby, nor without the two horns she carries strapped to her belt: one for signaling battle and one for drinking alcohol. Menial labor and farming bore her immensely, and she would rather be feasting, fighting, or raiding. That being said, when she gets sent to protect caravans that head to trade hubs (such as Cat's Cradle), Ry'kyna is known to get cantankerous and moody, with the end of any day she wasn't able to get into a fight being filled with a copious amounts of drinking.

At 6th Level: Ry'kyna the barbarian has gotten over her weariness of being a simple "guard dog" for the basic merchant caravans that travel along the trade routes of the region. Instead, she has come to realize that it is riskier roads or the wagons carrying the most valuable goods that incur the greatest possible chance of an ambush taking place … and that is the type of chaos and violence she wishes to test her mettle against. Having left the relative calm of protecting her own people, who were more than capable of defending themselves without her, Ry'kyna opts now for the most dangerous assignments. She is even part of a betting pool at the Brackish Moon Tavern in the Old Town District of Cat's Cradle: whichever mercenary brings the most fangs, ears, or fingerbones of things they've killed within a week gets free drinks all night.

At 10th Level: Ry'kyna of the Gray Wolves sits on the patio of a local tavern, wearing her worn mithril cuirass and with her weapons laid out on the table before her, as she angrily counts the coin remaining in her pouch. Anyone who keeps up with local rumor knows the tale: The barbarian woman has traveled far from her homeland back to Cat's Cradle in order to find the alchemist who sold her tribe cursed potions and salts that caused a plague to

lacking are overshadowed by the pure determination the Raven exhibits in ensuring a job gets done. While typically any job is open for them, there is still a code that is followed: no robbing or harming the poor and destitute, and no killing of innocents. While it cannot be proved, it is rumored that certain members of the city guard have taken to unofficially hiring the Raven to handle tough situations they find themselves stuck in. Proficient in tracking, thieving, and combat, their skills are always available to anyone who can pay the price. A designated offering box is in the temple of Valdyr where those wishing to meet the Raven can leave a written note proposing a business meeting.

At 10th Level: As the years have progressed, the Raven has become a master thief and a merciless killer. Because of the increase in their skillset, their loss of morality, and also because of the fact that they no longer remove their plague doctor mask under any circumstances, some say the current Raven is no longer the original elven rogue, and that the one that is rumored to be striking from the shadows throughout Cat's Cradle is really someone (or something) else that has simply taken up the mantle. Whether or not that is the case, the Raven still acts as a mercenary-for-hire and is willing to do any deed that requires theft, intimidation, maiming, or killing. No longer perturbed by the fact that they often get blamed for any random wonton deaths in the city and surrounding locales, the Raven seems to embrace their new moniker "Angel of Death" and uses this reputation to their benefit (either by getting more work or by intimidating payment out of scared individuals).

NO LONGER THE BIRD OF YORE

The original Raven has gone, but their mantle has been upheld by someone else, a very adept Yshkat rogue who uses the reputation previously built up by the original Raven to get work. If the players had any interactions with the original Raven, this new one does not remember nor honor any previous dealings. Whether or not the original Raven is somewhere still alive is up to your discretion.

decimate her people. No one has been able to help her, either because they are too afraid or because there have been no leads to help in the investigation. Ry'kyna has very little information to go on for her quest: a strip of black cloth with red threading, a fragment of a scroll with mysterious abstract runes written in blue ink, and a map of a cave system with no discernable markings. She is looking for anyone with information about curses, incurable illness, backfiring potions, or anything that can lead her to what she seeks.

Ry'kyna of the Gray Wolves, Female Human Barbarian (Ftr3): HP 21; AC 7[12]; Atk battle axe (1d8+2) or javelin (1d6+2); **Move** 12; **Save** 12; **AL** N; **CL/XP** 3/60; **Special:** +2 to hit and damage strength bonus, multiple attacks (3) vs. creatures with 1 or fewer HD, rage (6 rounds per day, −1 save penalty, +2 to hit and damage, immune to fear and charm). **Equipment:** leather armor, battle axe, wolf pelt.

Ry'kyna of the Gray Wolves, Female Human Barbarian (Ftr6): HP 42; AC 7[12]; Atk *+1 battle axe* (1d8+3) or javelin (1d6+2); **Move** 12; **Save** 9; **AL** N; **CL/XP** 6/400; **Special:** +2 to hit and damage strength bonus, multiple attacks (6) vs. creatures with 1 or fewer HD, rage (12 rounds per day, −1 save penalty, +2 to hit and damage, immune to fear and charm). **Equipment:** leather armor, *+1 battle axe*, wolf pelt.

Ry'kyna of the Gray Wolves, Female Human Barbarian (Ftr10): HP 61; AC 6[13]; Atk *+1 freezing battle axe* (1d8+3 + 1d6 cold) or javelin (1d6+2); **Move** 12; **Save** 5; **AL** N; **CL/XP** 10/1400; **Special:** +2 to hit and damage strength bonus, intimidating presence (1/day, 30ft range, one target is afraid as *fear* spell, save avoids), multiple attacks (10) vs. creatures with 1 or fewer HD, rage (20 rounds per day, −1 save penalty, +2 to hit and damage, immune to fear and charm). **Equipment:** *+1 leather armor*, *+1 freezing battle axe*, wolf pelt.

SARGASH UTHAK

Sargash Uthak is an up-and-coming mariner on Hyon Lake, captain of the trim schooner Doleful Wanderer and part-owner in several others. Flamboyant, outgoing, and loud, Sargash attracts others of his kind, who all have good hearts but little respect for the law. He revels in adventure, for though Hyon is well isolated from the high seas, it is nevertheless a dangerous place plagued by fearsome lake monsters and even its own breed of corsairs who prey upon the lucrative trade routes between Cat's Cradle and lakeside towns and villages.

At 3rd Level: Sargash himself has been sailing for nearly a decade, starting off as an assistant deckhand and cabin boy and rising through the ranks to become first mate of a large merchant ship. His background is somewhat spotty, including stints of smuggling and even an occasional flirtation with outright piracy when he lived on the seacoast years ago. Today he maintains a relatively lawful existence, but he is not above occasionally returning to his old ways, smuggling contraband in and out of Cat's Cradle, bribing the odd official or sabotaging competitors whom he feels haven't played him fair. Sargash's history is a bit spotty.

At 6th Level: Years on the lake have transformed Sargash into a veteran Hyon captain, with a small fleet of ships and crews of experienced sailors. He doesn't go out on trade runs as much as he used to but instead spends more time managing his business from his floating headquarters aboard the refitted *Doleful Wayfarer*. He maintains a love-hate relationship with the law, and still engages in questionable activities, but his basically good nature remains. Nevertheless, he has encountered a great deal of prejudice against non-humans and has been known to use these prejudices to his advantage, feigning murderous rages and threatening those who stand in his way. For the most part, his displays are all bark and no bite but usually succeed in getting Sargash his way.

Sargash has also become a more flamboyant character, dressing in feathered hats and sporting piratical weapons at his side, though he rarely uses them. He broke his tusks in an accident several years ago when he was struck in the face by an out-of-control boom. One of his tusks has been capped with gold, while the other he leaves broken and jagged as a reminder to him and his crews to always be wary.

At 10th Level: An aging, grizzled but still vital and often dangerous individual, Sargash continues to manage a large fleet of lake vessels and has grown quite prosperous. He is an even more powerful combatant. He has never married or had children, and continues to manage his business alone aboard the *Doleful Wayfarer.* Some of his current isolation and his drift away from his old goodhearted nature may be attributed to the fact that he now carries a secret curse.

During one of his increasingly rare expeditions across the lake to transport volatile and expensive alchemical reactants, Sargash was ambushed by a small fleet of corsairs in light, fast vessels who attempted to swarm the *Doleful Wayfarer* and plunder its valuable cargo. Sargash met the corsair's leader, a half-ogre with a fearsome blood-covered axe, in battle and prevailed despite near-mortal wounds. Upon recovery, Sargash took the axe as his own, never realizing that it was actually a *berserker axe* and that now he values it above all other possessions. Unaware of the axe's fearsome powers, Sargash led another voyage across the lake the following spring, with his first mate Synaela, a half-elven mariner, someone for whom Sargash had, for the first time, felt true love. As luck would have it, the *Wayfarer* was again attacked by corsairs, but as Sargash and Synaela fought side-by-side on the deck, he was wounded by a pirate and went berserk. He cut down Synaela before the attackers were finally defeated.

Grief-stricken, Sargash retained enough sense to realize the full horror of what had happened, and subsequent research proved to him that the axe was indeed cursed, yet he still cannot rid himself of it. He has determined never to go out on the lake again and to avoid combat at all costs, lest he inflict further tragedy on himself and others. His old goodness has been replaced by gruff wariness and increasing paranoia, though he still holds out a faint hope that someone will be able to rid him of his terrible curse.

Captain Sargash Uthak, Male Orc Sea Captain: HD 3; **HP** 15; **AC** 6[13]; **Atk** *+1 battle axe* (1d8+1) or spear (1d6); **Move** 9; **Save** 14; **AL** L; **CL/XP** 3/60; **Special:** none. (*Monstrosities* 364)
Equipment: leather armor, *+1 battle axe*, spear.

Captain Sargash Uthak, Male Orc Sea Captain: HD 6; **HP** 33; **AC** 4[15]; **Atk** *+1 battle axe* (1d8+1) or spear (1d6); **Move** 9; **Save** 10 (+1, ring); **AL** L; **CL/XP** 6/400; **Special:** none. (*Monstrosities* 364)
Equipment: *+2 leather armor*, *+1 battle axe*, spear, *ring of protection +1*.

Captain Sargash Uthak, Male Orc Sea Captain: HD 10; **HP** 57; **AC** 4[15]; **Atk** *berserker axe* (1d8+2); **Move** 9; **Save** 4 (+1, ring); **AL** L; **CL/XP** 10/1400; **Special:** none. (*Monstrosities* 364)
Equipment: *+2 leather armor*, *berserker axe* (cursed) (see sidebar), *ring of protection +1*.

Val Kaden

An attractive human in their late-30s leans up against the side of a covered wagon. A pale face with freckles and pinned-back brilliant curly red hair, they are wearing a smart leather jerkin, with matching leather skirt and boots, but it is their long multi-colored cape that draws your attention. Its swirling patterns make you think of the starry night sky, of a field of poppies and dandelions, of a rushing river, a thunderstorm, an explosion of fire. You blink your eyes and look up into their smiling face. "A silver for the show, love. And that includes one free drink!"

At 3rd Level: In their youth, Val Kaden was born into a nomadic tribe of con artists and deceivers that would perform false miracles, set up rigged games of chance, or even offer contrived fortune-tellings, all in the effort to fool the common folk of the land and steal the meager amount of money they

may have scraped together. With their naturally bright red hair and attractive features, the tribe had hoped to train them up to be a skilled con artist to woo marks out of their wealth. But Val had other plans. They wanted to travel the lands and let out into the world the music they heard in their soul. Instead of stealing from the folk they met, they would offer legitimate hope and uplifting moods. Ah, the naivety of youth. Years later, a down-on-their-luck Val found themselves in the city of Cat's Cradle performing at any inn or tavern they could in order scrape together enough to pay for a room and food. Always seeking work and keeping an eye for any odd jobs, they will always have a few rumors at the ready for things going on in or around town. During their time in Cat's Cradle, they picked up a few useful spells, although they never felt the desire to commit fully to the reclusive life of a wizard.

At 6th Level: Val Kaden is an established bard of moderate renown in the city of Cat's Cradle who performs occasionally at the more well-known establishments, even including a place or two in the Jade District, but can primarily be found at the Rebellious Boggart in the Gold District. Val themself has regained a level of optimism about the world and is always on the lookout to do a good deed to the downtrodden. While they would never go up directly against any of the criminal groups in Old Town, Val always seems to be able to direct city guard or do-good adventurers in a direction that would disrupt a criminal enterprise or the like. Occasionally Val leads a small group that they refer to as their "band" to do a bit of "adventuring" themselves outside of the city, typically if it comes to acquiring a lost or stolen object or fending off a troublesome creature harassing local farmers or mining groups. Most of the city guards appreciate this work that Val does and pass along leads or rumors that they cannot follow up on themselves.

At 10th Level: Val Kaden is now the leader of a roaming entertainment group calling themselves the "Exemplariliy Scramacious Twilight Troupe." While they still consider Cat's Cradle to be their "home" (for lack of a better term), the band travels tirelessly on all the surrounding roads and caravan routes: to Voles and Dancers to the north and south, and to Five-and-Copper and Sundry to the east and west. They entertain with their magic shows, acrobatic performances, feats of physical amazement, and humorous tales of adventure. Val makes sure that any "games of chance" offered by the troupe are not rigged in their favor and instead are a legitimate test of skill or wit. The troupe has acquired enough of a reputation that they are not mistaken for a band of thieves, but they still prefer to set up camp outside of most city walls, only entering town when obtaining food and supplies. Val makes sure to employ numerous scouts and hunters that protect the group when they travel, but they also serve as guards when they establish camp near a location

where coin can be obtained from the populace. When the troupe finds itself set up outside the walls of Cat's Cradle (which is often), Val occasionally pops into town to visit the Rebellious Boggart where they used to work and keeps a pleasant relationship with the owner. While Val does more managing and organizing these days, they do still occasionally perform as a special occurrence for particularly wealthy or invigorated audiences. Val is always willing to have an audience with almost anyone to hear whatever proposition they wish to present to them (or their troupe) but rarely do they seek anyone out themselves for any jobs.

Val Kaden, Human Performer (Thf3): HP 9; AC 7[12]; Atk scimitar (1d6) or dagger (1d4) or shortbow x2 (1d6); **Move** 12; **Save** 13; **AL** L; **CL/XP** 3/60; **Special:** +2 save bonus vs. traps and magical devices, backstab (x2), read languages, spells, thieving skills.
Spells: 1/day—*light, phantasmal force.*
Thieving Skills: Climb 87%, Tasks/Traps 25%, Hear 4 in 6, Hide 20%, Silent 30%, Locks 20%.
Equipment: leather armor, scimitar, dagger, shortbow, 20 arrows.

Val Kaden, Human Performer (Thf6): HP 17; AC 6[13]; Atk scimitar (1d6) or dagger (1d4) or shortbow x2 (1d6); **Move** 12; **Save** 10; **AL** L; **CL/XP** 6/400; **Special:** +2 save bonus vs. traps and magical devices, backstab (x3), read languages, spells, thieving skills.
Spells: 1/day—*detect magic, ESP, light, phantasmal force.*
Thieving Skills: Climb 90%, Tasks/Traps 40%, Hear 4 in 6, Hide 35%, Silent 45%, Locks 35%.
Equipment: *+1 leather armor*, scimitar, dagger, shortbow, 20 arrows.

Val Kaden, Human Performer (Thf10): HP 26; AC 4[15]; Atk scimitar (1d6) or *+2 dagger* (1d4+2) or shortbow x2 (1d6); **Move** 12; **Save** 8 (+2, cloak); **AL** L; **CL/XP** 10/1400; **Special:** +2 save bonus vs. traps and magical devices, backstab (x3), read languages, spells, thieving skills.
Spells: 1/day—*detect magic, ESP, light*; 3/day—*phantasmal force.*
Thieving Skills: Climb 94%, Tasks/Traps 70%, Hear 5 in 6, Hide 75%, Silent 80%, Locks 75%.
Equipment: *+1 leather armor*, scimitar, *+2 dagger*, shortbow, 20 arrows, *cloak of protection +2.*

VALDRIN HOFF

Valdrin is a serious and hard-bitten individual who rarely smiles, but who retains a deep sense of right and wrong. Orphaned in infancy, he grew up in a series of orphanages and workhouses, learning to survive by his wits and with his fists, while also gaining a deep understanding and affection for the lowly and the downtrodden in society. As a young man, he joined the city watch in a large city, only to be appalled by the corruption and uncaring attitude of his colleagues. After learning as many skills as he could — including learning multiple languages, gaining expertise with light crossbows, and the secrets of disabling hostile spellcasters — Valdrin quit the watch and made his way to Cat's Cradle, where he set himself up in the Ovens, providing security and aiding locals who were ignored by the city watch, particularly in the Ovens and the Old City.

At 3rd Level: Today, Hoff continues his trade, operating out of a small, rundown apartment. He has been instrumental in solving a number of important crimes throughout Cat's Cradle, but this is not widely known as he often prefers to hand out justice personally, rather than rely upon the city watch, whom he considers little better than the corrupt organization in his former home. On the other hand, Hoff and the members of the constabulary have developed a grudging mutual respect over the years. Hoff's contacts within the constabulary often share information with him and usually turn a blind eye to his extra-legal activities. For his part, Hoff allows some criminals to be taken into custody if supervised by the constabulary.

At 6th Level: The years have sharpened Hoff's reflexes and skills, as well as making him an especially feared nemesis of criminals across Cat's Cradle, especially the operatives of the Kennock Syndicate. After several run-ins, Hoff is determined to bring the Syndicate down whatever it takes and has even begun to pursue some of his own independent investigations of the organization's smuggling and protection schemes. He has forged a

close professional relationship with Inspector Mattea Theasean, who has been helping him surreptitiously and keeping her actions secret from her superiors.

Valdrin also shuns the use of magic and magical items in his investigations, though he has a number of spellcasting allies whom he turns to when needed. A recent job for a number of fey whose clan relic had been stolen also led to good relations with the fair folk, whom he also occasionally calls upon to aid him in his investigations. Prominent among his fey allies are Starshine, a mischievous but loyal and determined blue faerie dragon, and a band of sprites led by the warrior Daeg.

At 10th Level: At the height of his abilities and influence, Valdrin remains the defender of the common folk that he always was. His conflict with the Kennock Syndicate has grown into a full-scale war, and though a single investigator facing down with an entrenched criminal organization may seem like a one-sided and hopeless crusade, Valdrin soldiers on. Despite appearances to the contrary he is not alone, for he has his allies in the constabulary and his fey friends who have grown even more protective and loyal over the years. He has also developed a network of informers and assistants throughout the city of Cat's Cradle that includes beggars, shopkeepers, laborers and even a few petty criminals, all of whom keep him informed about the activities of the Thieves' Guild and the Kennock Syndicate, keeping him always a bare step ahead of those who wish to destroy him.

Valdrin Hoff, Freelance Investigator (Ftr3): HP 20; AC 7[12]; Atk 2 light crossbows (1d4+1) or longsword (1d8); **Move** 12; **Save** 12; **AL** N; **CL/XP** 3/60; **Special:** disguise, dual crossbows (−2 to-hit penalty with second attack), multiple attacks (3) vs. creatures with 1 or fewer HD.
Equipment: leather armor, longsword, 2 light crossbows, 20 bolts.

Valdrin Hoff, Freelance Investigator (Ftr6): HP 36; AC 7[12]; Atk 2 light crossbows (1d4+1) or longsword (1d8); **Move** 12; **Save** 9; **AL** N; **CL/XP** 6/400; **Special:** disguise, dual crossbows (−1 to-hit penalty with second attack), multiple attacks (6) vs. creatures with 1 or fewer HD.
Equipment: leather armor, longsword, 2 light crossbows, 20 bolts.

Valdrin Hoff, Freelance Investigator (Ftr10): HP 52; AC 5[14]; **Atk** 2 light crossbows (1d4+1) or longsword (1d8); **Move**

12; **Save** 5; **AL** N; **CL/XP** 10/1400; **Special:** disguise, dual crossbows (−1 to-hit penalty with second attack), multiple attacks (10) vs. creatures with 1 or fewer HD.
Equipment: chainmail, longsword, 2 light crossbows, 20 bolts.

Zoë Toranno

This full-bodied half-orc woman is made of pure muscle and intimidation. Her bronze skin glistens in the sun as she pulls the ship ropes off of the dock with a satisfied grunt. Her black mohawk stands prominently on its own, and the shaved sides of her head are tattooed with intricate purple and red designs. The necklace around her neck and the sleeveless, armored vest she wears are adorned with the fangs, claws, and bones of numerous predators she has slain in combat. Strangely though, on her left wrist she wears a single, unchained, manacle emblazoned with a faintly glowing triangular rune.

At 3rd Level: No one knows Zoe's original homeland, but many speculated based on her tales that it is far to the south where dragons are said to still roam free. Forced into servitude at a very young age, Zoë grew strong through manual labor and learned quickly about the cruelty of men in the world. After several years of captivity, she finally saw her opportunity to escape. When her captors failed to return after they left her in a desolate iron mine, she convinced her guards to abandon their duties, free her, and make for the nearest town. She doesn't talk about the journey to freedom, but she does tell people that she alone came out on the other end. A smart and strong woman needing to disappear and abandon the area, she signed onto a seafaring crew bound northward, and off she went. She jumped crews from time to time, making her way farther northward, before heading inland with a band of insurgents looking to unseat a local tyrant. Unsuccessful and on her own again, Zoë traversed the wilderness before coming across the town of Dancers. From there, she would eventually find herself in Cat's Cradle. Working the docks or signing up for a ship's crew, the strong half-orc woman was always up to any challenge. She is always willing to lend a helping hand to those who needed it and has vowed to fight against slavery and injustice whenever she encounters it.

At 6th Level: Zoë is well known throughout the Docks and Old Town of Cat's Cradle for her booming laugh and standoffish attitude. When she and whatever crew she is part of (usually a ship, but sometimes a caravan) arrive in town, they are known to rent out an entire tavern and offer to buy numerous

rounds throughout the night. She cares not for treasures or riches, just a good set of gear to fight her enemies, and more importantly, to defend those who cannot defend themselves. Zoë has a tense relationship with the guards of the city, as well as certain members of the criminal underworld, as she feels their living conditions and opportunities for honest work could always be better than what they currently are. She is always on the lookout to expose and stop corruption that she sees as a cancer spreading when left unchecked.

At 10th Level: As a captain aboard the boat *The Unchained Shark,* Zoë is one of the many who handles the imports and exports of the city via the waterways. She had earned a reputation of being honest and fair when it comes to her transporting and rates, and woe betide any who try to take them in a fight. Not only that, but she is known to take the *Shark* and go hunting for river pirates or bandit camps that have been established on the water's edge. A champion of the honest working classes and for the downtrodden, she has yet to ever retreat from a fight to which she has committed herself. In addition, Captain Zoë knows a lot about the locations along the length of the rivers of the region; whether it be ruins, caves, camps, or even strange landmarks, she can pass along her knowledge of them to those who have gotten into good graces.

Zoë Toranno, Female Half-Orc: HD 3; **HP** 12; **AC** 6[13]; **Atk** flail (1d8+1) or hand axe (1d6+1); **Move** 9; **Save** 14; **AL** L; **CL/XP** 3/60; **Special:** +1 to hit and damage strength bonus. (*Monstrosities* 364)
Equipment: ring mail, flail, hand axe.

Zoë Toranno, Female Half-Orc: HD 6; **HP** 29; **AC** 6[13]; **Atk** flail (1d8+1) or hand axe (1d6+1); **Move** 9; **Save** 14; **AL** L; **CL/XP** 6/400; **Special:** +1 to hit and damage strength bonus. (*Monstrosities* 364)
Equipment: ring mail, flail, hand axe.

Zoë Toranno, Female Half-Orc Ship Captain: HD 10; **HP** 54; **AC** 6[13]; **Atk** flail (1d8+6) or hand axe (1d6+6); **Move** 9; **Save** 14; **AL** L; **CL/XP** 10/1400; **Special:** +1 to hit and damage strength bonus. (*Monstrosities* 364)
Equipment: ring mail, *gauntlets of ogre power,* flail, hand axe.

Appendix A: New NPC Type

Master alchemists in the Salchamp are skilled in the uses of the various alchemical salts brought forth from the mines. These mages often set up shop and buy the salts from the miners so they can further their own studies into the unique properties of the reactive salts.

Master Alchemist (MU8): HP 25; **AC** 7[12] or 2[17] (missile) and 4[15] (melee) from *shield* spell; **Atk** staff (1d8); **Move** 12; **Save** 6 (+2, ring); **AL** N; **CL/XP** 8/800; **Special:** +2 save (spells, wands, staffs), spells (4/3/3/2).
Spells: 1st—*light, magic missile, read languages, shield;* 2nd—*levitate, locate object, wizard lock;* 3rd—*fly, hold person, slow;* 4th—*dimension door, remove curse.*
Equipment: robes, staff, *ring of protection +2,* pouch of alchemical salts (*darkness powder, incense of healing, water tablet*)*.
* See **Appendix B: New Items**

Appendix B: New Items

Alchemical Salts and Products

The so-called "salts" extracted from the strange formations of the Salchamp represent a variety of alchemical substances, many of which have proved valuable in the concoction of the unique substances crafted by Cat's Cradle's alchemists. While alchemicals can duplicate the functions of a range of magical potions, some have effects that differ significantly from their arcane counterparts. Listed below are several of the products whose manufacture is unique to Cat's Cradle, but these represent only a sampling of the many different alchemicals available in that city.

Darkness Powder. A more powerful version of *smoke powder,* a *darkness bomb* acts as a *darkness 15-foot radius* spell with a duration of one hour. Unlike the spell, it cannot be dispelled, but can be dispersed by wind or a breeze. 200 gp/vial

Enhanced Steel. This salve is applied to metals to temporarily improve their quality, though sometimes excessive use can have the opposite effect and damage or corrode the objects it is used on. A single treatment on a weapon gives it a +1 attack roll bonus for one full day. When used on armor, it provides a +1 bonus to AC for one full day. Effects of the salve are not cumulative, and further applications of the salve risk damaging it permanently. If a second application of *enhanced steel* is applied to an object that has already been treated, there is a 20% chance that the weapon or armor crumbles into dust. 100 gp/treatment

False Scent. Used by hunters and, less lawfully, by criminals being tracked by dogs or other scent-based creatures, false scent comes in small ceramic jars and can be applied to change the user's scent to a different creature, usually something benign such as a deer or rabbit. A single dose lasts one full day and protects its user from being tracked by any creature that uses scent. 50 gp/dose.

Incense of Healing. One of several different incenses sold in Cat's Cradle and created with Salchamp salts, a stick of *incense of healing* causes all creatures within 20 feet to regain 1d6 + 3 hit points. A stick must be burned completely for it to have this effect. 150 gp/stick

Incense of Silence. This incense takes 10 minutes to burn completely. During that time, a 20-foot radius is affected as if by a *silence* spell. The effect can be interrupted only if the incense is extinguished. 100 gp/stick

Incense of Tranquility. A stick of *incense of tranquility* takes an hour to fully burn, but provides the benefits of having rested through the night to all creatures within 20 feet. 200 gp/stick

Sleep Gas. This substance, usually found in a small glass vial, acts as a *sleep* spell when it is thrown at foes and breaks on impact. The spell affects all targets within a 20-foot radius, including friends and foes. 100 gp/vial.

Smoke Powder. A small vial of *smoke powder* acts as an *obscuring mist* spell when smashed on the ground with a duration of one hour and is dispersed by a moderate or stronger wind. 100 gp/vial.

Water Tablets. A single *water tablet* provides sufficient water to prevent the effects of thirst for up to eight hours. Smaller and far more compact than waterskins and other containers, *water tablets* are popular with adventurers, especially those who intend to venture into wilderness areas or far from civilization. 1 gp/tablet